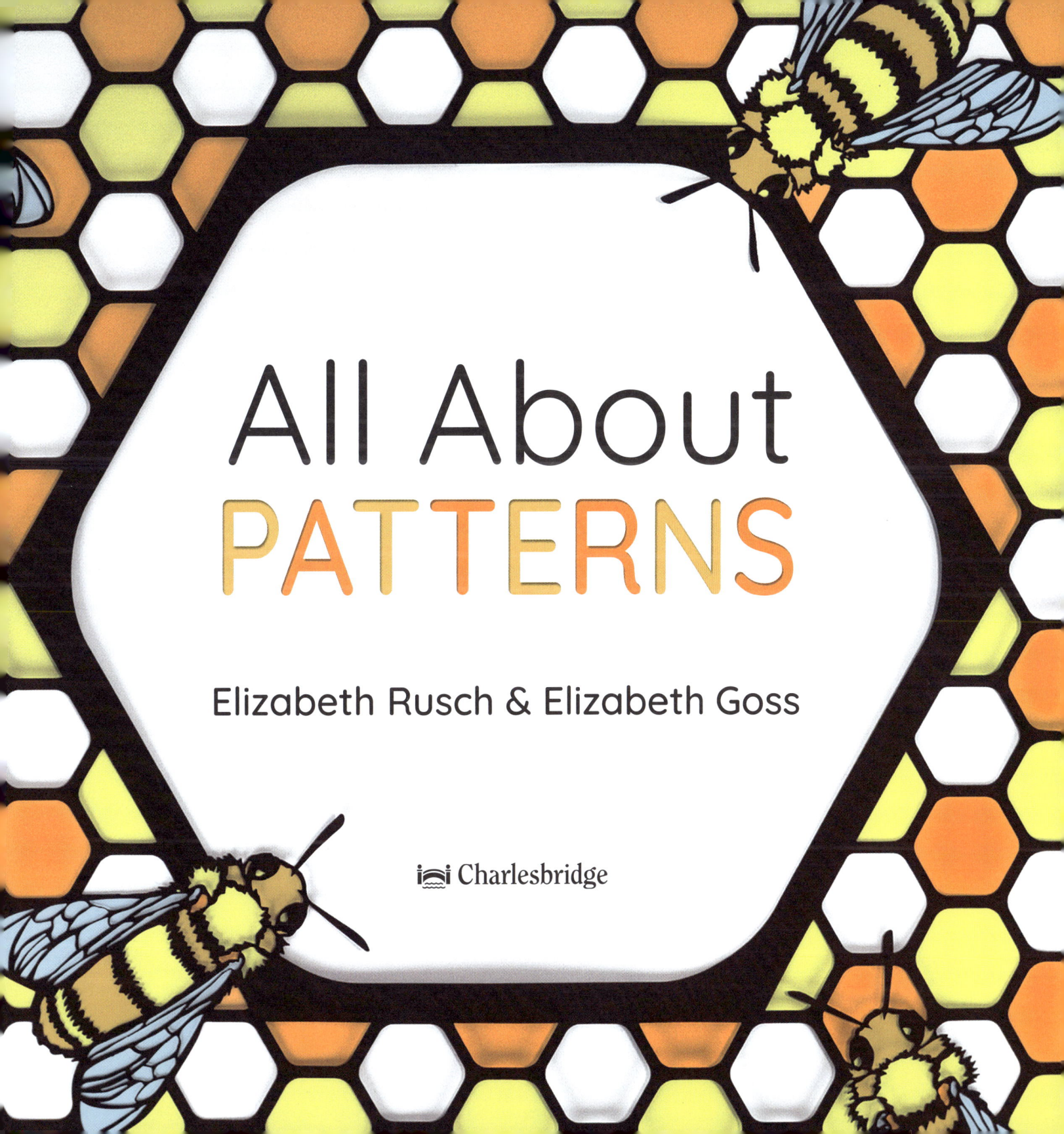

All About
PATTERNS

Elizabeth Rusch & Elizabeth Goss

Charlesbridge

What do you know about patterns?

Patterns are all about repeating.
Any objects, words, or sounds
that repeat over and over again
make a pattern.

Patterns spin. Patterns branch and even spread out like a star.

You can find patterns
everywhere and make patterns
with almost anything.

Even your feet,

your hands,

and your whole body!

Sometimes you can see a pattern
only when you're far away . . .

or up close.

Stories can have patterns,

and so can music,

with their different beats
and parts that repeat.

Once upon a

You might notice

a pattern to your day.

It helps you know
what happens next . . .

because color is light sending messages to your brain.

and when your favorite part is coming.

Sometimes when you break a pattern,

everything feels chaotic.

Until you find a way

to make a new pattern . . .

worth repeating!

MORE ABOUT PATTERNS

Our brains love finding patterns. What patterns can you find in the plants, animals, and rocks near your house, at school, or at the park? Do the windows, doors, or roof of your home make a pattern? Your floors, walls, or ceiling?

You can hear or feel patterns, too. Have you noticed parts of a song repeating? Have you read books with repeated words or images? How does that repetition make you feel? How do patterns help you predict what comes next?

Even your day can have a pattern: what you do when you wake up, what happens after lunch, how you wind down at night. What is your favorite routine? How does the pattern of your day change on the weekend or a holiday? Sometimes patterns can be comforting. Sometimes they feel boring. How could you change a pattern in your life to make your days more peaceful or more fun?

THE ART OF PATTERNS

Artists play with patterns, and so can you. Create your own pattern by drawing or stamping the same object—like a shape or an animal—over and over. The objects can go left and right, up and down, or in a diagonal. The repeating objects can even form a circle or a swirl, or burst out from the center like a firework.

As you play with patterns, see what happens if you make the repeating shapes bigger or smaller. Spread them out or squish them together. Draw lines across a paper and then fill in each section with a different pattern. Filling a whole page with patterns can look dramatic!

Some patterns are made up of shapes that fit closely together without any space between them. This tile-like pattern is called a tessellation. Artists make tessellations with all kinds of shapes!

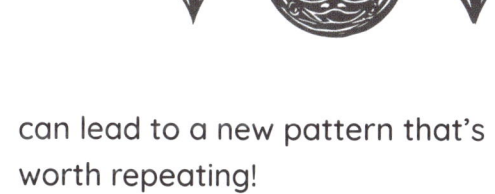

A pattern does not have to be perfect. In fact, a mistake in a pattern . . .

can lead to a new pattern that's worth repeating!

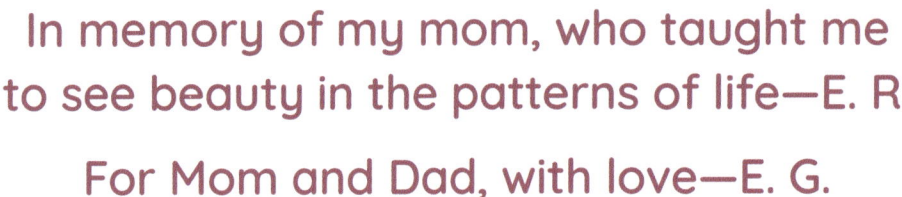

In memory of my mom, who taught me
to see beauty in the patterns of life—E. R.

For Mom and Dad, with love—E. G.

Published by Charlesbridge
9 Galen Street
Watertown, MA 02472
(617) 926-0329
www.charlesbridge.com

Printed in China
(hc) 10 9 8 7 6 5 4 3 2 1

Illustrations done in cut paper
Display and text type set in Quicksand by
    Andrew Paglinawan
Printed by 1010 Printing International Limited in
    Huizhou, Guangdong, China
Production supervision by Jennifer Most Delaney
Designed by Jon Simeon

Library of Congress Cataloging-in-Publication Data
Names: Rusch, Elizabeth, author. | Goss, Elizabeth
    Ames, 1987- illustrator.
Title: All about patterns / Elizabeth Rusch; illustrated
    by Elizabeth Goss.
Description: Watertown, MA: Charlesbridge, [2025]
    | Series: All about noticing | Audience: Ages 4-8 |
    Audience: Grades 2-3 | Summary: "This concept
    picture book explores the art, math, and emotion
    of patterns, encouraging young readers to see the
    world differently."—Provided by publisher.
Identifiers: LCCN 2023056537 (print) | LCCN
    2023056538 (ebook) | ISBN 9781623543549
    (hardcover) | ISBN 9781632893253 (ebook)
Subjects: LCSH: Pattern perception—Juvenile
    literature.
Classification: LCC BF294.R87 2025 (print) | LCC BF294
    (ebook) | DDC 152.14/23—dc23/eng/20240424
LC record available at https://lccn.loc.
    gov/2023056537
LC ebook record available at https://lccn.loc.
    gov/2023056538

Special thanks to Marlene Kliman, specialist in early
childhood mathematics, for her invaluable advice
and expertise. Thanks also to agent Fiona Kenshole,
editor Alyssa Mito Pusey, and designer Jon Simeon
for the fun and productive collaboration.—The Lizzes